GARFIELD'S
GUIDE TO DIGITAL CITIZENSHIP

A GARFIELD® GUIDE TO
SAFE DOWNLOADING
Downloading Disaster!

Garfield created by
JIM DAVIS

Written by
Scott Nickel, Pat Craven, and Ciera Lovitt

Illustrated by
Glenn Zimmerman and Lynette Nuding

Lerner Publications ◆ Minneapolis

This series will help you learn to stay safe and secure online, from playing games to downloading content from the internet. Use the resources and activities in the back of this book to learn more about cybersafety.

This content was created in partnership with the Center for Cyber Safety and Education. The Center for Cyber Safety and Education works to ensure that people across the globe have a positive and safe experience online through their educational programs, scholarships, and research. To learn more, visit www.IAmCyberSafe.org.

Illustrated by Lynette Nuding & Glenn Zimmerman
Written by Scott Nickel, Pat Craven, and Ciera Lovitt
Covers by Glenn Zimmerman

Visit Garfield online at https://www.garfield.com

Lerner Publications Company
An imprint of Lerner Publishing Group, Inc.
241 First Avenue North
Minneapolis, MN 55401 USA

For reading levels and more information, look up this title at www.lernerbooks.com.

Main text font provided by Garfield®.

Library of Congress Cataloging-in-Publication Data

Names: Nickel, Scott, author.
Title: A Garfield guide to safe downloading : downloading disaster! / Scott Nickel [and four others].
Description: Minneapolis : Lerner Publications, [2020] | Series: Garfield's guide to digital citizenship | Includes bibliographical references and index. | Audience: Ages 7–11. | Audience: K to Grade 3. | Summary: "Nermal finds a site where he can download a new movie online for free. But with the help of Dr. Cybrina, cyber safety expert, he learns that some things are too good to be true"— Provided by publisher.
Identifiers: LCCN 2019021159 (print) | LCCN 2019980994 (ebook) | ISBN 9781541572782 (library binding) | ISBN 9781541587489 (paperback) | ISBN 9781541583009 (pdf)
Subjects: LCSH: Garfield (Fictitious character) | Internet and children—Juvenile literature. | Internet—Safety measures—Juvenile literature. | Online social networks—Safety measures—Juvenile literature.
Classification: LCC HQ784.I58 N534 2020 (print) | LCC HQ784.I58 (ebook) | DDC 004.67/8083—dc23

LC record available at https://lccn.loc.gov/2019021159
LC ebook record available at https://lccn.loc.gov/2019980994

Manufactured in the United States of America
1-46545-47590-8/13/2019

DOWNLOADING DISASTER!

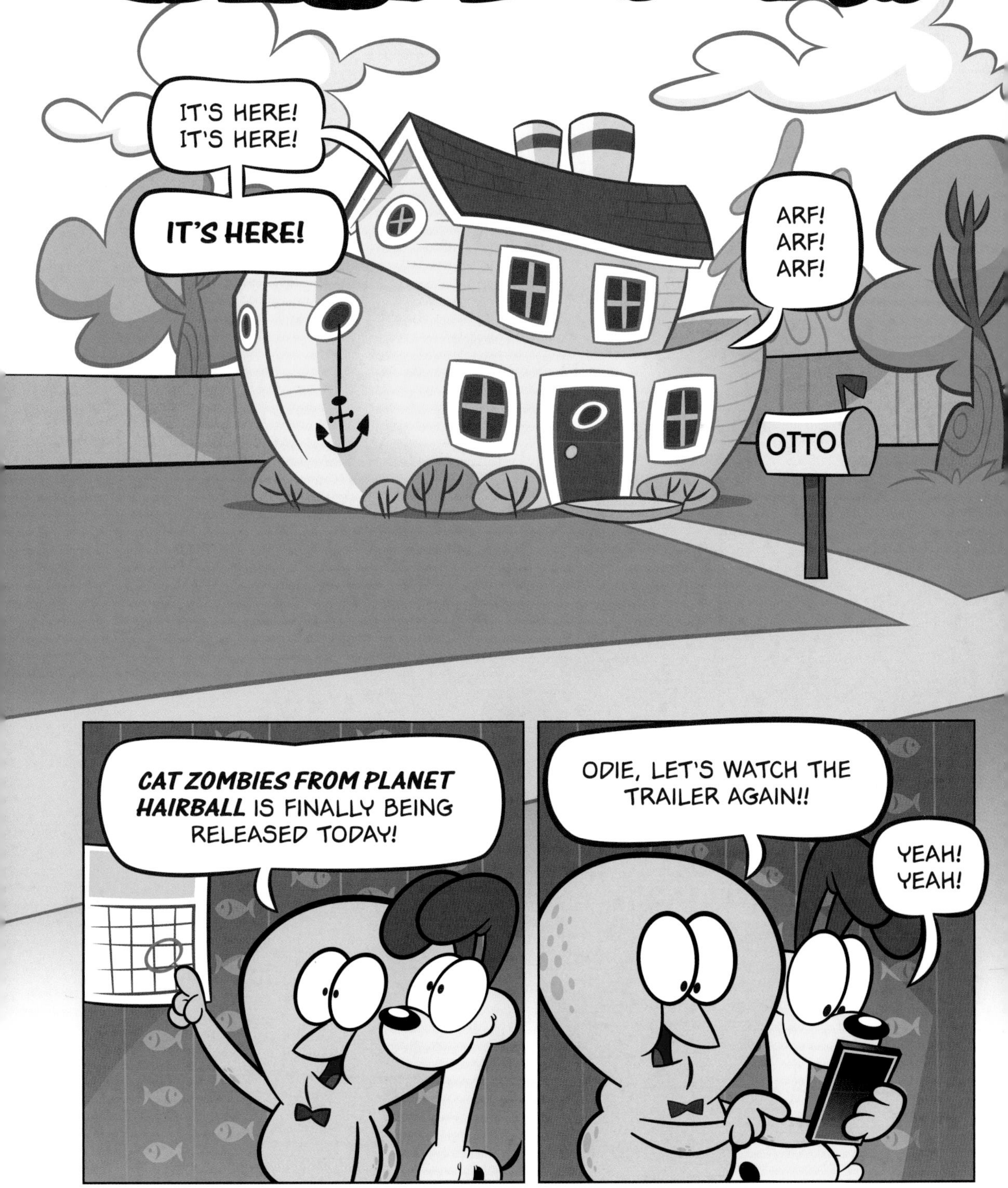

IT'S HERE! IT'S HERE!
IT'S HERE!
ARF! ARF! ARF!
OTTO
CAT ZOMBIES FROM PLANET HAIRBALL IS FINALLY BEING RELEASED TODAY!
ODIE, LET'S WATCH THE TRAILER AGAIN!!
YEAH! YEAH!

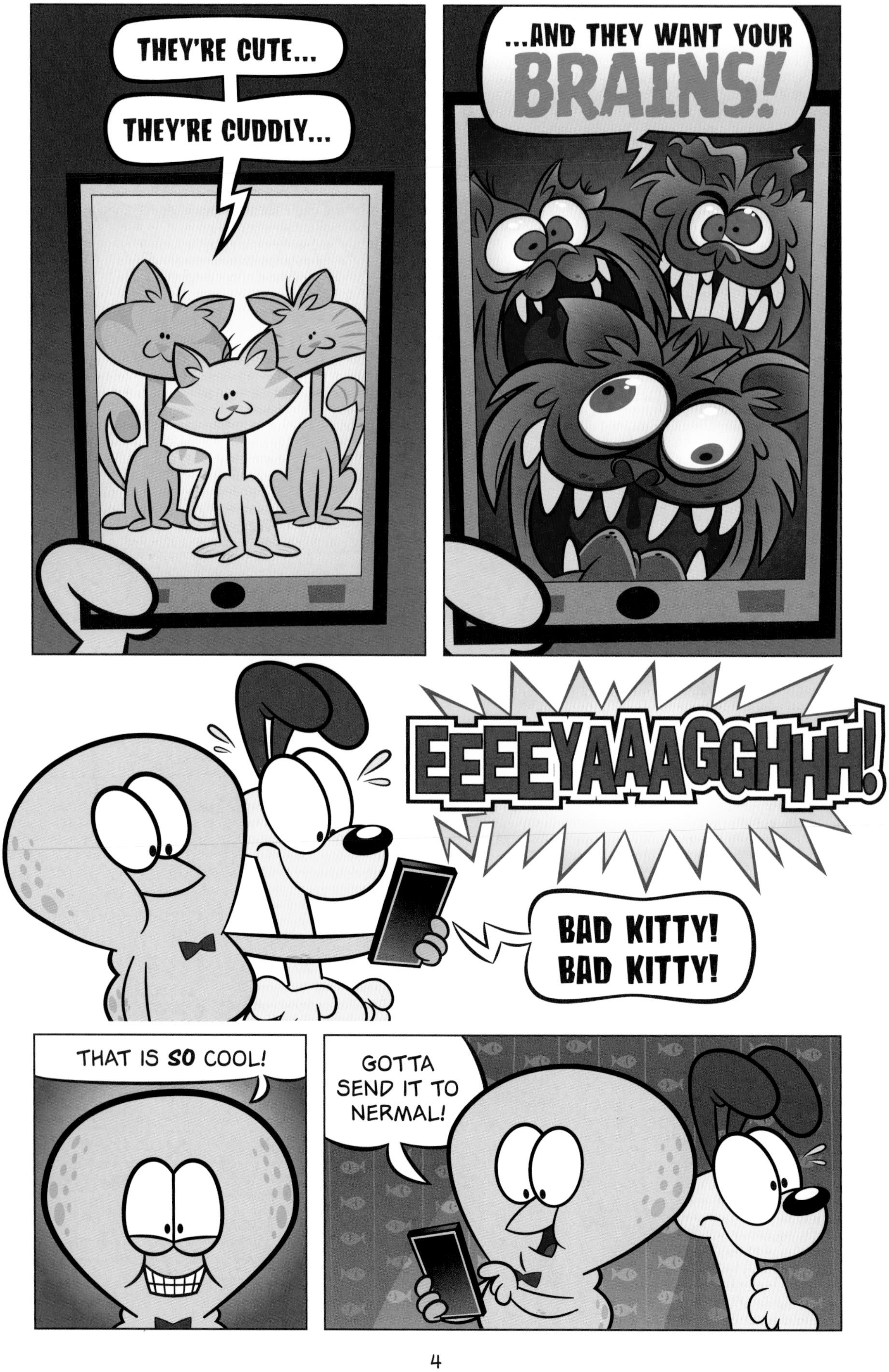

THEY'RE CUTE...
THEY'RE CUDDLY...
...AND THEY WANT YOUR BRAINS!
EEEEYAAAGGHHH!
BAD KITTY! BAD KITTY!
THAT IS SO COOL!
GOTTA SEND IT TO NERMAL!

SNIFFLE

PING!

MY PHONE...

THEY'RE CUTE... THEY'RE CUDDLY...

IT'S *ZOMBIE CATS FROM PLANET HAIRBALL!* SWEET!

R-R-R-R-ING!

INCOMING CALL OTTO

DUDE! THE MOVIE STARTS TODAY. WE HAVE TO GO SEE IT! ALL OUR FELLOW WARRIORS OF CHEESE ARE GOING!

ODIE TOO!

ARF!

SNIFFLE

SWEET! LET ME ASK IF I CAN GO TO THE MOVIES!

NO MOVIES.

BUT, ARLENE! PLEASE!

COUGH! COUGH!

SNIFFLE

NO, NERMAL. YOU HAVE A BAD COLD.

BUT I'M COUGH! FINE.

SEE?

I'M...

FINE.

PLOP!

SORRY, OTTO. NERMAL CAN'T MAKE IT.

THAT'S TOO BAD. NERMAL'S GONNA MISS ALL THE FUN.

UGH. I'M GONNA MISS ALL THE FUN!

COUGH! COUGH! COUGH!

NOW JUST STAY THERE AND **REST!**

I CAN'T SEE THE MOVIE WITH ALL THE GUYS. SNIFFLE

I'LL HAVE TO WAIT TILL NEXT WEEKEND AFTER EVERYONE HAS ALREADY SEEN IT!

OR... YOU COULD GO ONLINE **RIGHT NOW** AND **DOWNLOAD** THE MOVIE!

I CAN? YEAH!

OH NO! DOWNLOADING A FILM BEFORE IT'S OFFICIALLY RELEASED SOUNDS LIKE **STEALING!**

POOF!

POOF!

BUT IT'S NOT LIKE I'M GONNA **KEEP** THE MOVIE.

COUGH!

I'M JUST, UM... **BORROWING** IT!

THAT'S RIGHT!

WHY **WAIT?**

POOF!

OH, NERMAL!
PATIENCE IS A **VIRTUE**!

POOF!

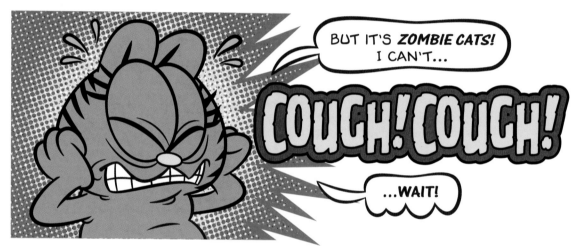

BUT IT'S *ZOMBIE CATS*!
I CAN'T...

COUGH! COUGH!

...WAIT!

OKAY, LET'S SEE... THERE ARE A
LOT OF **DIFFERENT** SITES THAT
SAY THEY **HAVE** THE **MOVIE**.

HERE'S ONE...
HMMM... THAT SITE
LOOKS A LITTLE SKETCHY,
BUT OH WELL...

TOTALLY SAFE! FREE! TOTALLY SAFE! FREE!
WATCH
ZOMBIE CATS FROM PLANET HAIRBALL
FREE! FREE! FREE!
CLICK HERE TO DOWNLOAD **NOW**!
FREE! TOTALLY SAFE! FREE!

LET'S DO
THIS THING!

BEEP!

WELL, THAT WAS EASY! *SNIFFLE*

PING!

DOWNLOAD COMPLETE. COOL!

HEY, WHAT'S THIS? IT LOOKS CHEAP, LIKE IT WAS FILMED IN THE THEATER!

ZOMBIE CATS FROM PLANET HAIRBALL

A VIRUS??! OH, NO!

VIRUS DETECTED!

RNING-WARNING-WARN

YIKES!

WARNING! WARNING!

SLAM!

GOTTA HIDE IT!

ARE YOU RESTING, NERMAL?

OH YEAH. JUST SITTING HERE. *SNIFFLE*

NOT DOING ANYTHING I SHOULDN'T.

DING! DONG!

EEK!

SETTLE DOWN, NERMAL. I'LL GET IT. IT MUST BE THE **PIZZA** I ORDERED.

WHAT? NO PIZZA?

IT'S A LETTER FROM THE **INTERNET PROVIDER.** IT SAYS THAT I **ILLEGALLY DOWNLOADED** A MOVIE AND THAT I MAY HAVE TO **PAY A FINE?**

THAT MEANS NO MORE MONEY FOR PIZZA!

NERMAL, WOULD YOU HAPPEN TO KNOW ANYTHING ABOUT THIS?

GULP!

I CONFESS! **I CONFESS!** IT WAS **ME!** I COULDN'T GO WITH MY FRIENDS TO WATCH **"ZOMBIE CATS FROM PLANET HAIRBALL!"** SO, I WENT ONLINE TO **DOWNLOAD IT!** I DIDN'T **KNOW** IT WAS GOING TO TURN INTO THIS BIG, FAT, HAIRY **MESS!**

I THINK THIS IS A JOB FOR **DR. CYBRINA.**

I'M ON IT!

BEE-YOOP!

CONTACTING DR. CYBRINA

AT THAT MOMENT, IN THE HEADQUARTERS FOR THE CENTER FOR CYBER SAFETY AND EDUCATION...

DR. CYBRINA, WE NEED YOUR **HELP!**

OH, HELLO, GARFIELD! SORRY, I WAS JUST DOING A LITTLE **JAMMING.**

SHREDDING CHORDS **RELAXES** ME.

IT'S ABOUT **DOWNLOADING** MOVIES ON THE INTERNET.

NO PROBLEM! AS A C.I.S.S.P.— CERTIFIED INFORMATION SYSTEMS SECURITY PROFESSIONAL— I'M ALWAYS ON THE JOB!

I JUST RECEIVED A **LETTER** FROM THE INTERNET PROVIDER SAYING I **ILLEGALLY** DOWNLOADED A MOVIE. BUT I **DIDN'T** DO IT. **NERMAL DID.**

OOPS! **COUGH! COUGH!**

DON'T WORRY, NERMAL. WE'LL GET THIS **STRAIGHTENED** OUT.

- DOWNLOADING MOVIES, TV SHOWS, AND MUSIC FROM BAD SITES IS STEALING, WRONG, AND COULD BE DANGEROUS.
- WATCH TV SHOWS AND MOVIES WHERE IT IS SAFE AND ETHICAL.
- USE CAUTION WHEN SEARCHING THE INTERNET FOR FREE THINGS.

LET'S TALK ABOUT WATCHING MOVIES AND TV SHOWS. THESE ARE VERY **IMPORTANT POINTS!**

12

NEVER DOWNLOAD MOVIES, MUSIC, AND TV SHOWS ON THE INTERNET FROM SOURCES YOU CAN'T TRUST OR DON'T KNOW. IT'S NOT SAFE AND IS ILLEGAL IN MOST PLACES. YOU COULD EASILY GET A **COMPUTER VIRUS** FROM THE BAD DOWNLOAD SITE.

BECAUSE DOWNLOADING TV SHOWS AND MOVIES FROM BAD SITES IS NOT ALLOWED IN MOST PLACES, THE INTERNET PROVIDER CAN SEND A **LETTER** TELLING YOU TO STOP ILLEGALLY DOWNLOADING. YOUR FAMILY COULD GET A FINE, OR YOU COULD **LOSE THE INTERNET.**

YIKES!

LUCKILY, THERE ARE MANY CHOICES FOR **WATCHING** OR **STREAMING** TV SHOWS AND MOVIES ON YOUR TELEVISION AND **OTHER DEVICES.**

BUT HOW DO **I KNOW** A SITE IS OKAY?

THAT'S AN **EXCELLENT** QUESTION, NERMAL. FOR TV, CHECK THE SHOW'S OFFICIAL **WEBSITE** FOR RECORDED EPISODES. TV SHOWS AND EVEN MOVIES CAN BE STREAMED **SAFELY** FROM MANY ONLINE SITES OR DEVICE APPS.

JUST **ASK** A PARENT, GUARDIAN, OR TRUSTED ADULT TO SEARCH WITH YOU TO FIND SAFE ONES. EVEN YOUR FAVORITE **GAMING SYSTEM** PROBABLY HAS MANY OPTIONS TO WATCH TV SHOWS, MOVIES, AND EVEN LISTEN TO MUSIC FOR **FREE.** SOMETIMES YOU MAY HAVE TO **PAY** FOR A SERVICE THAT ALLOWS YOU TO WATCH MANY SHOWS. SO AGAIN, MAKE SURE TO TALK TO A TRUSTED ADULT.

REMEMBER, EVEN **GOOD SITES** AND APPS MAY ASK FOR **PERSONAL INFORMATION** BEFORE YOU CAN STREAM THE VIDEO OR LISTEN TO THE MUSIC, SO IT'S ALWAYS A GOOD IDEA TO ASK AN ADULT TO HELP YOU DECIDE WHAT IS **RIGHT** AND **SAFE** FOR YOU.

THANKS, DR. CYBRINA. AS USUAL, YOU GAVE US **GREAT ADVICE.**

ROCK ON!

MY PLEASURE! NOW BACK TO MY **JAM...**

CLICK

AND SO, A FEW MINUTES LATER...

NERMAL, WE FOUND A GREAT **ONLINE** SITE WHERE YOU CAN WATCH LOTS OF MOVIES AND TV... ALL LEGALLY!

SO I WON'T GET ANY MORE LETTERS FROM THE INTERNET PROVIDER!

PETFLIX

IT'S A COOL **SITE** CALLED **PETFLIX!**

14

SWEET! SO I CAN **WATCH** *ZOMBIE CATS FROM PLANET HAIRBALL* ON PETFLIX?

NO, NERMAL. THAT'S A NEW MOVIE IN THEATERS. IT WON'T BE ONLINE FOR A WHILE.

BUT THERE ARE **LOTS** OF OTHER GREAT MOVIES AND TV SHOWS YOU CAN **WATCH.**

I'M PARTIAL TO THE COOKING SHOWS!

MY **FAVORITE** IS *EXTREME CUISINE: LASAGNA WARS!*

SPEAKING OF **LASAGNA,** I GOTTA RUN. IT'S TIME FOR MY POST-LUNCH-PRE-DINNER-MID-AFTERNOON **SNACK!**

WELL, I **GUESS** I'LL CHECK OUT WHAT'S ON PETFLIX. TOO BAD THEY DON'T HAVE **ZOMBIE CATS.** SIGH!

TAPPITY-TAPPITY-TAP

FORGET PETFLIX AND THEIR BORING LEGAL TV SHOWS AND MOVIES! LET'S SEARCH THE **INTERNET** FOR SOMETHING **REALLY GOOD**!

POOF!

COME ON! I BET WE CAN FIND **ANOTHER** SITE THAT HAS **ZOMBIE CATS** OR EVEN...

HEY!

NO THANKS.

PLINK!

POOF!

16

I'M **GLAD** HE'S **GONE!**

I'M VERY **PROUD** OF YOU!

POOF!

NOW LET'S WATCH SOME TV.

COOL! LET'S SEE WHAT'S ON PETFLIX. HEY, **WHAT'S THIS?** ZOMBIE CATS FROM PLANET HAIRBALL— THE PREQUEL??

PETFLIX ORIGINAL
ZOMBIE CATS
FROM PLANET HAIRBALL
THE PREQUEL

I'VE NEVER **SEEN** THIS. SU-WEET!

I CAN WATCH IT **OVER AND OVER AGAIN** AND TELL MY FRIENDS NOT TO **SPOIL** THE NEW **ZOMBIE CATS** MOVIE UNTIL I CAN SEE IT!

THE ONLY THING WE NEED NOW IS SOME **POPCORN!**

17

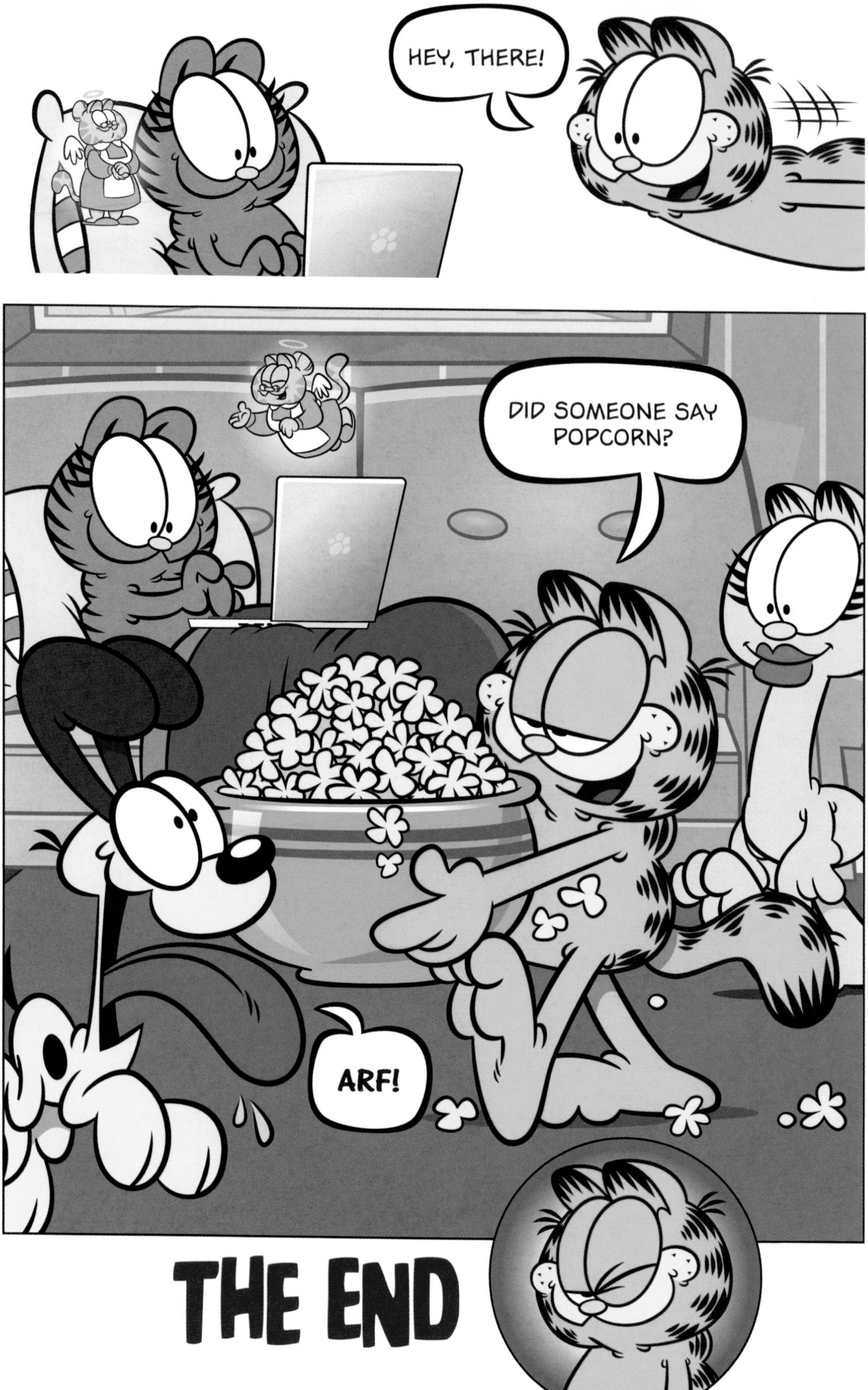
HEY, THERE!
DID SOMEONE SAY POPCORN?
ARF!
THE END

ACTIVITY: DOWNLOADING DISASTER

PART 1: DOWNLOADING MOVIES, TV, AND MUSIC

YOU WANT TO MAKE SURE THAT YOU DOWNLOAD A MOVIE FROM A SAFE, TRUSTED SITE. MARK YOUR ANSWERS ON A SEPARATE SHEET OF PAPER.

1. **What can happen if you download a movie from a bad site?**

    A. Your computer can get a virus.

    B. Your personal information can be stolen.

    C. Your family can have its internet connection taken away.

    D. Your family may have to pay fines.

    E. All of the above.

2. **What are signs that the site you are visiting is a bad site?**

   A. It's not the official TV show website.

   B. It's not a service that your family subscribes to for streaming movies, TV, or music.

   C. The site has movies still in the theaters.

   D. The site is asking you to download software in order to download movies, TV, or music.

   E. All of the above.

3. **When you watch a movie, TV show, or listen to music on the internet, what should you do?**

   A. Ask a trusted adult for a safe option.

   B. Search the internet, find it, and download it.

   C. Ask your friends what they use and do it too.

   D. Ask a friend to download it and send it to you.

4. **What should you do if you want to watch your favorite show on the internet?**

   A. Check the TV station's official website for recorded shows.

   B. Download it illegally if you have antivirus software on your computer.

   C. Find a streaming application online and use that.

   D. Search the internet and download the first one you see.

Congratulations! You just completed part 1. Let's look at the answers and see how you did!

PART 1: DOWNLOADING MOVIES, TV, AND MUSIC ANSWERS

HERE ARE THE ANSWERS TO THE QUESTIONS ABOUT SAFE DOWNLOADING OF MOVIES, TV, AND MUSIC.

1. **E. All of the above.**

   If you download a movie from a bad site, your computer can get a virus, your personal information can be stolen, your family can have its internet connection taken away, and your family may have to pay fines.

2. **E. All of the above.**

   You can tell you are on a bad site if it's not the official TV show website; it's not a service that your family subscribes to for streaming movies, TV, or music; the site has movies still in the theaters; or the site is asking you to download software to download movies, TV, or music.

3. **A. Ask a trusted adult for a safe option.**

   When you watch a movie, TV show, or listen to music on the internet, be sure to ask a trusted adult for a safe way to do so.

4. **A. Check the TV station's official website for recorded shows.**

   Always be sure to check the TV station's official website for recorded shows. You can also use a streaming service that is approved by a parent or guardian.

Excellent work!
You're on your way to becoming
a cybersafety superstar!

YOU'RE DOING GREAT! NOW LET'S ANSWER SOME QUESTIONS ABOUT DOWNLOADING AND STREAMING—AND HOW TO KEEP SAFE!

PART 2: TRUE OR FALSE

ARE THESE STATEMENTS ABOUT DOWNLOADING AND STREAMING TRUE OR FALSE? WRITE YOUR ANSWERS ON A SEPARATE SHEET OF PAPER.

1. You, a parent, or a guardian can get in trouble for your actions.

2. You need to stream videos and music illegally to get them for free.

3. If you don't plan on sharing the movie with others, then it's okay to download it illegally.

4. If a movie is still in theaters, it's likely not available for streaming safely.

5. If you have made a mistake and downloaded illegally, you should tell a parent or guardian right away.

6. If you've downloaded a movie from a bad site, your computer is probably fine if you haven't noticed anything wrong.

PART 2: TRUE OR FALSE ANSWERS

1. You, a parent, or a guardian can get in trouble for your actions.

True. Streaming movies, TV shows and music should be done ethically, or you and your family could get in trouble.

2. You need to stream videos and music illegally to get them for free.

False. Remember, there are safe and free options.

3. If you don't plan on sharing the movie with others, then it's okay to download it illegally.

False. Even if you don't plan on sharing the movie, it's not okay or safe to download from a bad site.

4. If a movie is still in theaters, it's likely not available for streaming safely.

True. Most movies that are still in theaters cannot be watched on the internet safely.

5. If you have made a mistake and downloaded illegally, you should tell a parent or guardian right away.

True. Trust your parent or guardian to help you.

6. If you've downloaded a movie from a bad site, your computer is probably fine if you haven't noticed anything wrong.

False. Tell a parent or guardian right away. A virus may have been sneakily downloaded at the same time.

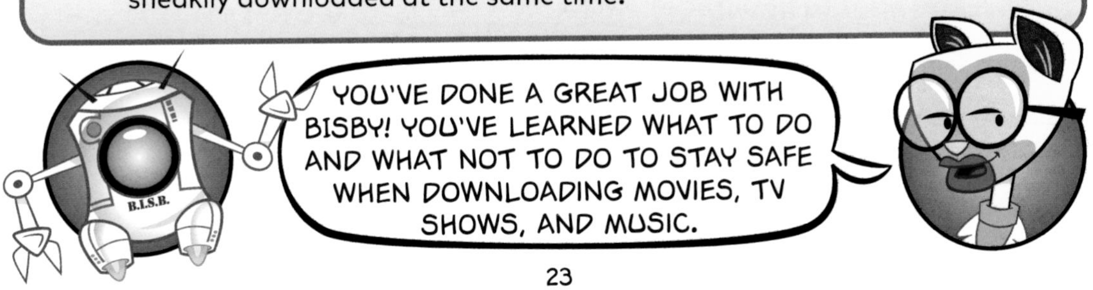
B.I.S.B.
YOU'VE DONE A GREAT JOB WITH BISBY! YOU'VE LEARNED WHAT TO DO AND WHAT NOT TO DO TO STAY SAFE WHEN DOWNLOADING MOVIES, TV SHOWS, AND MUSIC.

LET'S PUT THE KNOWLEDGE WE NOW HAVE ABOUT SAFE DOWNLOADING TO USE.

PART 3: FILL IN THE BLANKS

Which terms from the word bank best complete the sentences? Write down your answers on a separate sheet of paper.

WORD BANK

website	right	fines
download	online	computer
streaming	steal	movie
illegal	trusted adult	
official	virus	

1. Always use a trusted _____ or app for _____ movies, TV shows, or music.

2. Downloading from bad sites is _____ in most places and is not the _____ thing to do.

3. You should never _____ to watch your favorite shows or listen to music.

24

4. Talk to a _____ about safe streaming and get help if you've made a mistake.

5. Downloading illegally can cause your family to lose the internet, pay _____, or even break your _____.

6. Your computer could get a _____ if you _____ a TV show from a bad site.

7. If a _____ is still in theaters, you probably cannot stream it legally _____.

8. You might be on a bad site for watching TV shows if it is not the _____ website for the show.

YOU DID REALLY GREAT! KEEP THESE ANSWERS IN MIND, AND YOU'LL BE ABLE TO SAFELY DOWNLOAD AND STREAM MOVIES, TV SHOWS, AND MUSIC.

You go! You are officially an ONLINE SAFETY SUPERSTAR EXTRAORDINAIRE!

B.I.S.B.

B.I.S.B.

PART 3: FILL IN THE BLANK ANSWERS

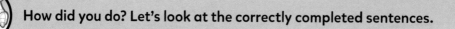

How did you do? Let's look at the correctly completed sentences.

1. Always use a trusted _____WEBSITE_____ or app for _____STREAMING_____ movies, TV shows, or music.

2. Downloading from bad sites is _____ILLEGAL_____ in most places and is not the _____RIGHT_____ thing to do.

3. You should never _____STEAL_____ to watch your favorite shows or listen to music.

4. Talk to a _____TRUSTED ADULT_____ about safe streaming and get help if you've made a mistake.

5. Downloading illegally can cause your family to lose the internet, pay _____FINES_____, or even break your _____COMPUTER_____.

6. Your computer could get a _____VIRUS_____ if you _____DOWNLOAD_____ a TV show from a bad site.

7. If a _____MOVIE_____ is still in theaters, you probably cannot stream it legally _____ONLINE_____.

8. You might be on a bad site for watching TV shows if it is not the _____OFFICIAL_____ website for the show.

NOODLE ON IT!

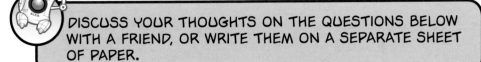

DISCUSS YOUR THOUGHTS ON THE QUESTIONS BELOW WITH A FRIEND, OR WRITE THEM ON A SEPARATE SHEET OF PAPER.

1. What are some safe streaming sites that you know about for watching movies and TV shows? What about for listening to music?

2. Why is it important to use safe sites to watch movies and TV shows?

3. What should you do if a friend wants to download a movie illegally?

4. What is the difference between streaming and downloading?

5. What are some ways you can keep yourself safe when watching TV shows and movies online?

INTERNET SAFETY TOOLBOX

1. **Keep personal information private and do not share it online or in-game.**

2. **If something makes you feel uncomfortable, log off and tell an adult.**

3. **Think before you click, send, or post.**

4. **Create strong, unique passwords, and never share them.**

5. **Get permission before tagging and posting pictures of other people.**

6. Report cyberbullying immediately.

7. Never meet an online-only friend without talking to a parent or guardian.

8. Follow age rules for social media sites and games.

9. Build safe profile pages, and make sure that your settings are set to private.

10. Remember that online friends are not the same as real friends.

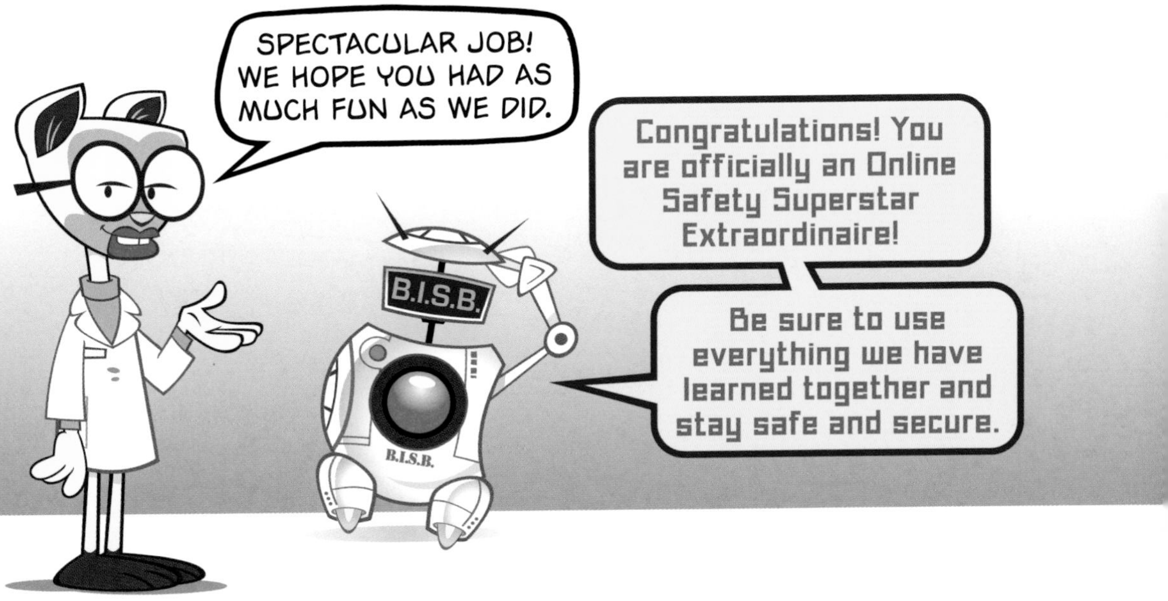

SPECTACULAR JOB! WE HOPE YOU HAD AS MUCH FUN AS WE DID.
Congratulations! You are officially an Online Safety Superstar Extraordinaire!
Be sure to use everything we have learned together and stay safe and secure.
B.I.S.B.

GLOSSARY

cyber: related to computers and the internet

download: to transfer data from one location, such as the internet, to another, such as a computer hard drive

information systems: systems that interpret and organize information

internet provider: a company that provides access to the internet

personal information: information that can help to identify a particular person

streaming: transferring from the internet in a continuous stream that is immediately played

virus: a computer program that harms a computer by destroying data or damaging software

FURTHER INFORMATION

Anton, Carrie. *Digital World: How to Connect, Share, Play, and Keep Yourself Safe*. Middleton, WI: American Girl, 2017.

Being Safe on the Internet
https://kidshelpline.com.au/kids/issues/being-safe-internet

5 Internet Safety Tips for Kids
https://www.commonsensemedia.org/videos/5-internet-safety-tips-for-kids

Hubbard, Ben. *My Digital Safety and Security*. Minneapolis: Lerner Publications, 2019.

Lyons, Heather, and Elizabeth Tweedale. *Online Safety for Coders*. Minneapolis: Lerner Publications, 2017.

Secure Password Tips from ConnectSafely.org
http://www.safekids.com/tips-for-strong-secure-passwords/

Explore more about Cyber Safety at www.IAmCyberSafe.org

INDEX